The Grandma Book

TODD PARR

Megan Tingley Books
LITTLE, BROWN AND COMPANY
New York   Boston

ALSO BY TODD PARR:

The Grandpa Book

The Daddy Book

The Mommy Book

The Family Book

It's Okay to Be Different

The Peace Book

The Feel Good Book

Reading Makes You Feel Good

Underwear Do's and Don'ts

Otto Goes to Bed

Otto Goes to the Beach

Otto Goes to Camp

Otto Has a Birthday Party

Otto Goes to School

A complete list of all Todd's titles and
more information can be found at www.toddparr.com

Little, Brown and Company

Time Warner Book Group
1271 Avenue of the Americas, New York, NY 10020
Visit our Web site at www.lb-kids.com

First Edition: April 2006

Library of Congress Cataloging-in-Publication Data

Parr, Todd.
  The grandma book / by Todd Parr. — 1st ed.
  p. cm.
  "Megan Tingley Books"
  Summary: Presents the different ways grandmothers show their
grandchildren love, from offering advice and babysitting to making things
and giving lots of kisses.
  ISBN 0-316-05802-5
  [1. Grandmothers—Fiction. 2. Grandparent and child—Fiction.] I. Title.
PZ7.P2447Gr 2006
[E] — dc22   2004027846

10 9 8 7 6 5 4 3 2 1

TWP

Printed in Singapore

This book is dedicated to my Grandma Parr. Some of my fondest memories are of her baking and her special cookie drawer. But my fondest memories of all are of the Christmas gifts of underwear and socks, which were at least five sizes too big.

And to my Grandma Logan, who has always been such a big part of my life. We talk every Sunday and she gives me ladybugs for good luck. Thanks for always being there for me and believing in me even when I didn't believe in myself. Thanks for reading GREEN EGGS AND HAM, over and over and over.

I love you very much.
Love,
Todd

Some grandmas have a lot of cats

Some grandmas have a lot of purses

Some grandmas give you
a lot of advice

Some grandmas give you a lot of books

Some grandmas help their neighbors

Some grandmas help take care of their grandchildren

Some grandmas like to make you eat a lot

Some grandmas like to
make you things

All grandmas like to

hear from you

Some grandmas like to dance

Some grandmas like to play bingo

Some grandmas live with a grandpa

Some grandmas live with
their friends

Some grandmas drive slowly

Some grandmas drive fast

All grandmas like to

give you lots of kisses

Grandmas are very special! They make sure you are warm and safe and that you always have a full tummy. They know everything. Tell them you love them every day. ♡Love, Todd

Rosketyn